Lust and Law

by

Autumn B. Tate

ONE

"I'm ending this affair with you, Elizabeth, and staying with my wife, Samantha! I'm going to the police today, and I'll tell them you're the one who's responsible for the death of our managing partner's wife. You killed Jennifer! Jennifer was your very own fraternal twin sister! Elizabeth, you killed the only woman I loved!"

"If you go to the police, Attorney Lawrence Wilcox, I'll tell everyone you were having an affair with Jennifer, the wife of George Hawkins, the head honcho of our law firm. If you want to keep your job, and if you don't want your wife Samantha to divorce you, you'd keep your damn mouth shut!"

"You're blackmailing me again, Ms. Jones?"

"You're damn right I am!" hollered Elizabeth. "If I go down, you go down with me! You can kiss that associate position of yours goodbye! Two hundred thousand yearly salary, all down the drain! Butler, Sterling & Burgess can find another lawyer just like you! Chicago, Illinois, is full of lawyers! You're nothing special here in Chicago!"

"Insult me all you want, Elizabeth! I'm done with you. The hot sex is over!"

"You'd better be glad I never contacted your wife Samantha and told her you were screwing me and my sister Jennifer."

"Oh," Lawrence replied with a curious look in his eyes. "Another threat of blackmail, huh, Elizabeth? Going to run and tell Samantha about my sexual indiscretions?"

"Relax, Lawrence. I've got bigger fish to fry than you and your marriage to Samantha. I've never met her. You've shown me pictures of Samantha on your cell phone. Attractive woman, indeed, although not as attractive as I am." Elizabeth chuckled with conceit, feeling very envious of Samantha's attractiveness.

"Are you done flattering yourself at the expense of my wife Samantha? If you are, I'm going to get back into my white Mercedes right over there and drive to a police station and let them know there is a killer on the loose named Elizabeth Jones!"

Just as 28-year-old Sarah Romans rolled down her window to catch a breeze as she ate her tasty breakfast in the law firm's underground parking lot, she overheard this fiery exchange between her colleagues that changed the course of her Monday.

Sarah was stunned by what she'd just heard. The words of her co-workers were just as hot as the sizzling July sun.   Sarah's frantic heart raced. Her mind was overwhelmed, and she never expected she'd overhear the startling details of sex, murder, adultery, and blackmail.

Why, Sarah never imagined she'd be resigning from Butler, Sterling & Burgess law firm on a day like this, but everything that had been unfolding at work, including the intense exchange between her two co-workers in a nearby car, clearly revealed it was time for Sarah to part ways with the law firm immediately.

TWO

She Works Hard for the Money blasted inside Sarah's car as she drove into her law firm's underground parking lot twenty minutes ago. Sarah had never heard the Donna Summer song before. The '80s hit was before Sarah's time, but the beat and lyrics resonated with her.

Tired of working hard for the money and getting no respect, Sarah finally quit her receptionist job at Butler, Sterling & Burgess. She could no longer take the egomaniacs and was ready to say goodbye to 250 South Wacker Drive, the downtown Chicago home of the medical malpractice law firm.

South Wacker Drive had plenty of law firms, yet none quite like Butler, Sterling & Burgess. Why, this was the first time Sarah had ever heard of a local law firm having its very own announcement of a murder suspect---all courtesy of Lawrence and Elizabeth.

Sarah couldn't believe the news she heard about the law firm she once held in high esteem. Sarah fondly remembered her first day at the firm, filled with excitement. The staff was friendly, the office's ambiance was mesmerizing, and the firm's popularity was far-reaching, with associates and partners from Butler, Sterling & Burgess often featured on local and national news.

Sarah reflected on her journey to this firm and Chicago as she thought about the disturbing news from Elizabeth and Lawrence. As soon as this Sioux Falls, South Dakota native with stunning red hair and dark brown freckles graduated from the University of South Dakota with a liberal arts degree, she sent resumes to local companies in Sioux Falls. However, they all turned down Sarah, saying she was overqualified or lacked experience.

Sarah decided to expand her horizons and emailed resumes to several companies and firms in several states, including Illinois. She wanted to fulfill her dream of moving to the Windy City, so she sought employment wherever she could despite the months of frustration she had endured.

Bethany Owens, the human resources coordinator for Butler, Sterling & Burgess and a proud native of Sioux Falls, South Dakota herself, was impressed with Sarah's determination and drive, having seen Sarah's cover letter and resume on the very day she posted the receptionist ad on the law firm's website. Sarah's resume was impressive, and her cover letter highlighted her 4.0 GPA, her two-time election wins as the University of South Dakota student council president, and the weekly tutoring sessions she conducted with elementary students. Sarah was an academic rock star.

Through Sarah's stellar resume and cover letter, Bethany reminisced about her college experiences at the University of South Dakota ten years ago. Bethany told herself she'd grab any opportunity to help bright applicants reach their highest potential. Sarah is a bright applicant, a fellow graduate of the University of South Dakota, and a fellow South Dakotan.

Three hours after submitting her resume and cover letter to Butler, Sterling & Burgess and going through a Skype interview from her bedroom in her parents' home, Sarah accepted Bethany's job offer as the receptionist and a moving allowance to help Sarah relocate.

Butler, Sterling & Burgess hardly offered a moving allowance to support staff, but Bethany made an exception in Sarah's case. Bethany felt Sarah's experiences, intelligence, positive attitude, and willingness to go the extra mile were assets the law firm could use. Bethany told Sarah that if she ever decided to advance from the receptionist role, she would be helpful in other capacities. The law firm would love to have her.

Such an invitation was delightful to Sarah, for Sarah's parents took her and her older brother Walter to Chicago, the "Windy City," for a family vacation when Sarah was eight and Walter was ten; her childhood memories of Chicago—of the Sears Towers, of eating ice cream, popcorn, and hot dogs at the White Sox's baseball game, and of visiting the Chicago Zoo—all stayed with Sarah as she grew up. *This is my kind of city. I can't wait to move here,* Sarah thought as she and her family cherished the fun.

But that was then, and this was now. Even though Sarah loved the big city thrills of Chicago, her adoration for Butler, Sterling & Burgess had significantly faded. Butler, Sterling & Burgess was constantly in the news for its victories in multi-million-dollar lawsuits. Sadly, though, as the firm's success inflated, so did the staff's egos. Sarah could no longer take the pompous attitude.

After being subjected to repeated blatant disrespect from arrogant attorneys, demeaning words from some staff, and a salary she had outgrown, Sarah felt she had to go. The handwriting on the wall was clear: it was time to spread her wings and fly to greater heights, especially after hearing that a co-worker was a suspect in the murder of the managing partner's wife. Such daunting details only fueled Sarah's desire to cut all ties with this firm.

Besides Sarah's plans to resign, the only other thing on her mind before she heard the shocking chat in the other car was sitting inside her car and relishing her morning breakfast. From Monday to Friday, like clockwork, Sarah loved stopping at Ralph's Deli, one of Chicago's favorite eateries, to get her hefty breakfast of tasty food.

Sarah's workday commute started with a morning trip to the deli. It was the highlight of her day. After turning off the blaring alarm clock at 6 a.m., she'd brush her teeth, wash her face, shower, and get dressed. She'd rush out of her apartment at 6:55 a.m. and arrive at Ralph's Deli no later than 7:30 a.m. It took only 10 minutes to get her order—either a toasted turkey bacon bagel sandwich or a toasted turkey patty sandwich with toppings, or on rare occasions, pancakes, hash browns, egg whites, or sunny-side-up eggs.

Being on time for her 8:15 a.m. to 5:15 p.m. receptionist job was important to Sarah. Punctuality meant a lot to her and the firm. During Sarah's interview with the firm, she was told the law firm had zero tolerance for tardiness. That's the reason the eight previous receptionists had been fired. When Butler, Sterling & Burgess said the start time at work was 8:15, it didn't mean 8:16, 8:18, or 8:20. Excellence was the middle name of this law firm.

But that was fine. Sarah didn't have a problem getting to work on time. She timed everything just right so she could enjoy some alone time enjoying her morning breakfast seated in her car in the underground parking lot just before hearing Lawrence and Elizabeth's fiery chat; while nibbling on her breakfast in her car, Sarah recollected snippets of her telephone chat with her boyfriend of one year. Just before dozing off last night right after talking to her boyfriend, Jeffrey Edwards, a 28-year-old junior accountant at a downtown Chicago accounting firm, Sarah decided she'd resign without giving a two-week notice.

"Sarah, you know I care about you and support whatever you do, but baby, are you sure you're making the right decision to quit Bulter, Sterling & Burgess? Do you want to quit your job?" Jeffrey asked.

"What else can I do, Jeffrey? Every time I wake up in the morning and rush to work now, I get a terrible ache in my stomach."

"You're sure that's not indigestion?" Jeffrey joked.

"No, Jeffrey, it's not. Butler, Sterling & Burgess is no longer the place for me. My time there is over. As soon as I get to work tomorrow, I tell my boss I'm quitting."

"Okay. You have my full support, babe," replied this handsome, suave Chicago native with the dashing looks of Hollywood heartthrob Zac Efron. "You need me to stop by your office for encouragement?"

"Thanks, but no thanks," Sarah replied.

"Sure?" Jeffrey asked. "Why not?" He frowned.

"Some battles a lady has to fight alone."

Sarah was grateful for her boyfriend's encouragement and appreciated his concern. Jeffrey's kindness, care, and understanding were among the traits she loved about him and what drew her to him when they first met. Seated next to each other at a Chicago White Sox baseball game, having never met before, Sarah and Jeffrey struck up a conversation and realized they had two things in common: their love for baseball and the fact that they had arrived at this sporting event alone, having been stood up by their respective dates.

The excitement of the baseball game caused Sarah and Jeffrey to get a little too carried away with their cheers and screams as the White Sox beat the Tampa Bay Rays 11 to 4. Sarah and Jeffrey accidentally bumped into each other and knocked their beers out of each other's hands from celebrating just a tad bit much.

Both offered to buy the other another beer, but Sarah and Jeffrey declined. Instead, they smiled, blushed, and exchanged phone numbers. Two days later, the budding lovebirds went on their first date and exchanged warm kisses and embraces.

Sarah was happy her love life was in a good place, but she was uncertain about the direction of her career. She was optimistic, though, that she could find another job in no time with the money she'd saved while working at the law firm and the professional contacts she'd made since arriving in Chicago. Staying at the law firm was no longer an option. Sarah was ready to move forward to the next chapter of her life.

As Sarah glanced at her car's clock, she counted the minutes before taking the elevator to the 20th floor to see her supervisor, Thomas Alex, one last time and inform him she was leaving the law firm. Still staring at the clock, Sarah sighed as she thought today would be an unconventional day, the last of many firsts. These thoughts roamed through her mind just before she rolled down her car's window and overheard Lawrence and Elizabeth's startling conversation.

Today would indeed be the last time Sarah would enter this parking lot and see the smiling faces of the weekday parking attendants. It would also be the last time she would taste the delicious meals in the law firm's cafeteria. Why, today would mark the end of memorable moments at the firm.

That was the course Sarah was willing to take. Still, in the six years she had worked for the vast firm, she'd never imagined she'd be filled with such sadness. Her sadness quickly turned into anxiety, though, the moment she heard Lawrence and Elizabeth exchange some cars away.

THREE

Sarah's attention was fixated on the spat between Elizabeth and Lawrence. She could not have ignored their ranting even if she tried, for they'd hollered loudly.

Sarah had looked forward to rushing upstairs to see her supervisor and informing him she was resigning. However, hearing the unexpected breaking news from Elizabeth's car delayed her plan and nearly caused her to choke on her food.

Sarah had wanted to sit inside her car while eating breakfast and listening to the radio. Yet, after hearing the shocking revelations from Lawrence and Elizabeth, she suddenly lost her appetite for food, lively music, and the comedic banter of WKLT's popular morning radio co-hosts. Without further hesitation, Sarah attempted to turn on her car's engine and rush out of the parking lot for fear of learning any additional details regarding Lawrence and Elizabeth's affair and Jennifer's murder.

Sarah accidentally hit her car's horn, alerting Lawrence and Elizabeth that someone else was in the parking lot. In her desperate attempt to escape, Sarah gained unwanted attention. *How could I have been so clumsy? How could I have been such a klutz? That happens when you've worked at a law firm like this for years. I've been turned into an uncoordinated melted jellybean.*

Exposed, Lawrence and Elizabeth looked around as they remained seated inside Elizabeth's Jeep Cherokee, struggling to discover who may have heard them. Lawrence and Elizabeth were so engaged in their riveting chat they'd forgotten they'd rolled down their windows.

In the heat of the moment, their voices scaled. As Elizabeth and Lawrence turned their heads and looked in Sarah's direction, they immediately saw Sarah quickly bending her head forward so as not to be seen.

Sarah had no idea she'd stumble upon this alarming news, especially on a day like today when she had plans to quit the firm. It's true that when the employees of the firm heard the managing partner's wife, Jennifer, had been found dead in her husband's office eight months ago, they were in shock.

It turned out Attorney Lawrence Wilcox, a second-year associate in the firm, had been carrying on an extramarital affair with Jennifer until the day she died. No one had known of Jennifer and Lawrence's affair except Elizabeth, the estranged fraternal twin sister and the culprit of Jennifer's death. Suddenly, though, Sarah was privy to what happened, and having been found out by Elizabeth and Lawrence, she was anxiously scrambling for cover.

FOUR

On the night Jennifer was found dead in her husband George's office, all indications pointed to her husband George as the culprit. The initial investigations landed him in jail on suspicions it was he who had murdered his wife so that he could get the twenty-five million dollars from her life insurance policy.

The investigations had led to criminal charges, with George facing life in prison if convicted. For the past eight months since Jennifer was killed, George had been in jail in pre-trial detention and had remained there even today----the first day of his criminal trial for first-degree murder.

District Attorney Walter Higgins admitted the evidence against George was largely circumstantial. Yet, with the testimonies from witnesses, including Elizabeth's, and the findings of their lengthy investigations, the outcome of the trial would indeed prove beyond a reasonable doubt George had the ability, motive, and vicious intent to murder his wife, Jennifer.

Throughout George's ordeal, Lawrence had remained silent about his affair with Jennifer. It was Lawrence and Jennifer's secret until Elizabeth unexpectedly got wind of it. What started as a simple hello at the firm's summer yacht party three weeks after Lawrence was hired two years ago quickly became a steamy affair between Lawrence and Jennifer.

The 60-year-old stunningly handsome managing partner of Butler, Sterling & Burgess, George Hawkins, had hosted the annual social outing aboard his yacht for the past ten years. That night, the five-million-dollar expansive and exquisitely designed yacht was filled with chosen law firm staff members, George, and Jennifer's elite friends.

Stepping aboard the magnificent cruiser, Lawrence felt he had arrived as he stood with his attractive wife, Samantha, and made small talk with the staff and guests. George personally invited Lawrence to attend the function and told him to bring his wife, Samantha.

When George first met Lawrence, he saw himself in this vibrant, intelligent, ambitious, and handsomely tanned man. George and Lawrence had distinct similarities: natives of Manhattan, New York; married to an attorney; were an only child; lovers of tennis, golf, and soccer; smokers of an occasional cigar; and avid connoisseurs of Greek, Lebanese, and Mediterranean cuisine. George's father was a famed New York City criminal attorney, and Lawrence's mother was an acclaimed New York City divorce attorney, and George and Lawrence shared a love for the law. One might say being a lawyer was in their DNA or was their destiny.

On the day George invited Lawrence to the summer party aboard his yacht, Lawrence couldn't wait to share the news with his wife, Samantha. Ecstatic, Lawrence, and Samantha looked forward to attending the grand event. They even went shopping together to pick out matching outfits.

When Lawrence and his wife Samantha were first introduced to Jennifer by George at the summer yacht party, Lawrence was immediately drawn to Jennifer's beautifully styled brunette hair, fashion flair, and sexy face and body. Jennifer's physique made Lawrence think of a Hollywood actress his mother often talked about and loved: Andie MacDowell. In Lawrence's mind, Jennifer and Andie could pass for identical twins.

Jennifer felt attracted to Lawrence and tried hard to conceal it until the moment was right. Even though Lawrence was just 25 years old at the time, 35 years younger than Jennifer, the age difference between the two did not matter. It only intensified their sexual attraction.

Although Jennifer was sixty, she could have quickly passed for half her age. Diet, exercise, and retail therapy were her tricks for staying youthful. Lawrence had never dated older women, even though he'd always been attracted to them.

Never one for turning down an opportunity to sow his wild oats if the escapade suited his erotic taste for women, Lawrence didn't want to miss a chance to enjoy Jennifer's flesh. Lawrence and Jennifer were whisked away into their world of titillation.

When Jennifer slipped into the unisex single-stall restroom on the lower level of the yacht, Lawrence subtly followed her, hoping to engage her in conversation when she exited. When Jennifer opened the restroom door to return upstairs, she was surprised to see Lawrence standing there. She winked and smiled at him. Ready to release her attraction for Lawrence, Jennifer turned her head and saw no one was around; she discreetly invited Lawrence into the lavishly spacious restroom, quickly shutting the door as their passion for each other was ignited.

Jennifer hurriedly unbuttoned Lawrence's shirt, almost causing a tear, and Lawrence unzipped Jennifer's dress as their hands, mouths, lips, and genitalia turned into sensual tools satisfying their sexual thirst. As their clothes fell to the floor, so did their naked bodies. Briskly moving from the sink to the marble floor, Lawrence and Jennifer kissed as their tongues and hands devoured each other.

Lawrence called out Jennifer's name, and Jennifer called out his. Jennifer loved the way Lawrence's penis moved inside her vaginal walls. The way Lawrence sucked her breasts was beyond words. His tongue tickled the nipples of her breasts, then slid downward, upward, and then around and around her body.

Lawrence paused to study Jennifer's face to see if she wanted more pleasure. The more Jennifer took in his licks and sucks, the more her nipples and clitoris both stood at attention. Jennifer had never had her sweat-soaked body ingested in such a manner, even by her husband George, and thought at any minute she would implode. If Jennifer had collapsed under the power of Lawrence's tongue, hands, and penis, she'd have awakened and begged Lawrence for more.

As Lawrence and Jennifer's sexual acts intensified, so did their panting. Not wanting to stop, their orgasmic thrusting went on and on until they both peaked with pleasure.

As Jennifer and Lawrence rested in each other's arms while lying on the floor of the yacht's restroom, still stark naked, Jennifer turned to look at Lawrence. She said, "I dated a handful of men before I met my husband George and married him, but none of them clung to my body and ravished me with their hands, lips, tongue, and penis the way you have, Lawrence. No man has ever made love to me like that. I can't get enough of you!" She added, "Truthfully, I haven't made love like that with any other man, not even my husband George."

"I'm just the man for the job, then." Lawrence leaned in and kissed her soft lips.

"You want to do this again?" Jennifer asked with a smile. "We've been in here for at least thirty minutes. I'm sure your wife and my husband are wondering where we are. We'd better compose ourselves and return to the party upstairs."

"I want to see you again, Jennifer. I want to do this again," Lawrence said with laughter.

"I look forward to it. I can't wait!"

"Just tell me when and where, and I'll be there to satisfy you in all the ways you want."

"One favor deserves another," replied Jennifer. "I want to please you, too, Lawrence. I'm many things, but I'll never be sexually selfish whenever it comes to you."

"You did a superb job of satisfying me; you can be sure of that," replied Lawrence with a grin.

"The suck you gave my cock sent me into another world. I can't wait to go there again with you."

"I feel the same way, Lawrence."

"I'm all in, baby. I'm all in for you, Jennifer."

FIVE

Lawrence and Jennifer's stolen moments of passion were constantly repeated during their two-year romance. The two did all they could to hide their affair, often meeting in hotels for breakfast, lunch, dinner, or dessert in the mornings, afternoons, and evenings.

When they couldn't be together, they texted each other salacious messages, made spicy phone calls to each other, and even sent naked pictures and naked videos of themselves to each other via phone. With each passing day, week, and month, their sexual rendezvous became more frequent, and their sexual secret remained successfully hidden until the day Elizabeth found out about it.

Jennifer was the managing partner at Smith & Harpers, another medical malpractice law firm in downtown Chicago. The firm's office was only two blocks from Butler, Sterling & Burgess. The two firms' convenient locations made it easier for Jennifer and Lawrence to sneak away and feast on each other.

From the moment Lawrence heard about Jennifer's mysterious death, he had been devastated and heartbroken. It boggled his mind why anyone would want to kill such a caring, sensual, vulnerable, and compassionate woman like Jennifer, whom Lawrence had grown to care about during their time together genuinely. He couldn't imagine anyone wanting to end the life of the woman of his dreams. Something inside Lawrence told him, however, George wasn't responsible for Jennifer's death.

Lawrence envied how George spoke of Jennifer when George introduced Jennifer to Lawrence and Samantha at the firm's summer yacht party. Lawrence could tell George was a man who was madly in love with his wife. Lawrence had hoped he'd feel the same about his wife Samantha when he reached George's age. Only time will tell.

Jennifer often reflected on her life with her husband as her emotions for Lawrence intensified. Even though George was outspoken, strong-willed, sarcastic, high-strung, playful, and critical at times, he was enthusiastic about three things: his marriage to Jennifer, their children, and the law. George was a genius when it came to the law, which initially drew George and Jennifer together: their fascination with the law and each other.

George and Jennifer met at Harvard Law School during their first year and soon began dating. Months after they graduated from law school, they relocated to Chicago, where Jennifer and Elizabeth lived. George and Jennifer both had passed the bar and began to practice law at their respective law firms in Chicago. Jennifer went to work at the Smith & Harpers law firm, where she was employed until she was murdered, and George took a job at Butler, Sterling & Burgess and worked his way up from being an associate to a partner to the managing partner, just as Jennifer had also done at the law firm where she worked.

A year after their first employment, George and Jennifer exchanged marriage vows in a small but humble wedding. It was a grand day on which they promised each other forever. They stayed married for over 30 years until Jennifer's death.

Sixteen years into their marriage, at the respective ages of forty-two, Jennifer and George announced they were having twins, and nine months later, Jennifer gave birth to Anna and Abigail. As both George and Jennifer had always wanted to adopt a child, one year later, one-year-old Jonathan was added to the Hawkins family via adoption. Now, their family was complete. Sounds of laughter, singing, and family time constantly filled the Hawkins' home. The Hawkins family was the envy of many, and so was George and Jennifer's marriage.

Anna, Abigail, and Jonathan had remained in the family's stately 8.1-million-dollar home with eight bedrooms, six bathrooms, an indoor swimming pool, and an outdoor basketball court, nicely nestled in one of Chicago's exclusive neighborhoods. With George being away in jail, awaiting his trial, both his two older sisters—Darlene and Stephanie—relocated to Chicago from Dallas, Texas, to help buffer the blow of Jennifer's loss to her family, especially her children.

Since their mother's death, Abigail, Anna, and Jonathan had been shedding tears whenever they thought about their mother and how much they missed her. Although the loss of their mother was painful for them, the children appreciated their aunts' presence and were grateful for their kindness and company.

Uncertain their father had been the one who killed their mother but hoping he was not, Abigail, Anna, and Jonathan stayed open to hearing the evidence and prayed for an innocent outcome for their father.

SIX

During the times Lawrence and Jennifer were at a hotel for their sexual encounters, Jennifer often told Lawrence how much she adored her children. Abigail, Anna, and Jonathan meant the world to her. Jennifer loved her children but couldn't say the same about her husband, George. Throughout the years, Jennifer felt emotionally starved and sexually unfulfilled in her marriage.

What was once a union with sex twice a day had become a union with sex only once every two months, on weekends, and the weekly date nights had become mere memories. The spark and tingle Jennifer felt whenever George was around had faded into nothingness. When George walked through the front door after a long day at work, Jennifer often turned her head in disinterest as George tried to kiss her.

Jennifer no longer felt any attraction for George, even though she could tell George still deeply longed for her. Jennifer wondered in silence if this would always be the state of her marriage. Would she ever get back her passion for George? How did things become like this, and should she even care?

Jennifer sought answers for why her feelings and desires for George had declined. From seeking advice from her physician to determine if her diminished affection for George was hormonally based, to meeting with a therapist to unravel her lack of emotional attachment to even speaking with a member of clergy---to get some insights---despite not being a profoundly religious person herself, Jennifer wanted to know what brought about the change. She genuinely wanted answers. *Maybe, just maybe, knowing what brought on the change, my romantic and sexual affections for George might return.* Jennifer often pondered in silence.

On the day Jennifer and George were driving together in the family's newest Mercedes to attend the law firm's summer yacht party—the same day Lawrence and Jennifer first met and had their first sexual rendezvous—Jennifer was still searching for a way to rekindle their marriage. The rekindling never happened. Jennifer took one look at Lawrence and knew she wanted him. . . all of him . . . and only him. Jennifer wanted Lawrence in her life, atop her body, inside, beneath, and inside her heart.

It wasn't easy for Lawrence to leave his wife, Samantha, considering they were newly married when he first met Jennifer. Lying in bed next to Lawrence after one of their sexual escapades at a downtown Chicago hotel, Jennifer thought to herself as she stared at Lawrence while he slept, *Would Lawrence leave his wife Samantha to be with me? Lawrence told me he loved me, and I believe and love him, but are we ready to walk away from our marriages?* These were often Jennifer's inner thoughts.

Are my romantic feelings for Lawrence enough to tell George I want a divorce? I don't know. Maybe I should live in the moment and enjoy the way Lawrence holds me, kisses me, nibbles at my breasts, gives me oral pleasure, and sways and moves inside of me whenever we make love.

Lawrence loves it when I please him sexually. He loves the way I caress his solid shoulders and then move my lips to kiss them. I'm overwhelmed when he releases loud moans whenever I give him oral pleasure and whenever he's deep inside me. Lawrence always begs me for more, and I can't help but say yes. We're like fire every time our bodies meet . . . fire that never needs quenching.

On rare occasions, Lawrence would mention the difficulties of his marriage to Jennifer, and Jennifer would do the same about her marriage with George. To Lawrence and Jennifer, their time together often felt like a life jacket . . . a life jacket meant to save them from drowning in parts of their marriages . . . the parts they didn't want to face . . . the parts that felt empty, lonely, barren, and lifeless—the parts they desperately wanted to escape.

Lawrence often reflected on his time with Jennifer whenever he was alone. Three days after Jennifer's death, as Lawrence was driving outside Chicago into the countryside to clear his head, he reminisced about a conversation he and Jennifer had just after making love at a popular bed & breakfast. The bed & breakfast pillow talk took place one year after their first sexual rendezvous aboard George's yacht. The romantic dialogue was forever etched in Lawrence's mind because the details gave Lawrence a window into Jennifer's emotional world with her husband.

"I love the way you hold me, Lawrence," Jennifer said as they cuddled in the king-sized bed & breakfast bed just after making love.

"I love the way you hold me, too, Jennifer."

"I can't promise you forever, Lawrence. I wished I could, but I can't," Jennifer said as she stared deeply into his eyes.

"I never asked you to," replied Lawrence. "How could I when I'm still married myself?"

"How long can we keep this up?" Jennifer asked as she tenderly kissed Lawrence on the lips.

"As long as you want me, I'm here, Jennifer. When you want to end this, tell me. Honestly, I don't know if I can walk away from you. I thought I could after the first time you and I had sex aboard the yacht at that summer party when we first met."

"I always think about that. We had sex inside that restroom. It was wild, with mad passion."

"I know . . . trust me, I know." He laughed as he kissed her lips.

"We'll just have to enjoy these moments and not worry about the future."

"Let's just let the future take care of itself."

"Yeah," Jennifer replied with a smile. "I agree. Since I met you, Lawrence, I've grown madly in love with you. My love and desire for my husband George is gone. I have nothing inside for him anymore. You are the only man I want, Lawrence."

A year after that conversation at the bed & breakfast—on the night of their second anniversary, Jennifer was found dead on the floor of her husband's office. The night of Lawrence and Jennifer's second anniversary was going to be quite memorable because they had made plans to have dinner together after meeting with their spouses and telling them both they wanted a divorce.

Jennifer was ready to tell George she and Lawrence had been having a sexual relationship and wanted to run off together and wed. Lawrence knew Samantha would be hurt after hearing he wanted to leave her for another woman, but he was ready to take that risk. Yet the dinner never took place, and neither did the confessions. With Jennifer's sudden death, Lawrence and Jennifer's romance ended unexpectedly.

What started as mere lust had slowly evolved into their heartfelt connection with each other. Lawrence missed Jennifer and her tender touch. He missed her smile, laughter, soft skin, and especially the intense legal exchanges they often had before, during, and after sex.

SEVEN

As the investigations into Jennifer's death got underway, Elizabeth concealed two things: her familial ties to Jennifer, which George himself didn't know, and she was the one who had killed Jennifer by triggering Jennifer's asthma attack and not coming to her aid when Jennifer during the attack.

Jennifer never told George about Elizabeth. Jennifer never felt she had to since she was estranged from Elizabeth. After being away from each other since the age of eighteen, when Elizabeth joined the Air Force, Elizabeth and Jennifer were both stunned to see each other again when they did. Elizabeth served in the military mainly to be with her high school sweetheart, who had also enlisted in the Air Force.

Shortly after enlisting in the Air Force, Elizabeth and her boyfriend broke up, but Elizabeth stayed in the military. Jennifer, however, headed to Massachusetts to attend Harvard University after being awarded a four-year academic scholarship.

Six months ago, however, after serving as a recruiter for the Air Force in Indianapolis, Indiana, for ten years, after her honorable discharge from the military, Elizabeth returned home to Chicago in search of employment. She wanted to try something new and different, so she applied for the executive assistant position she saw on a job portal.

Butler, Sterling & Burgess had been around 98 years and had become a heavy hitter in Chicago's legal community. Elizabeth felt with her strong work ethic and military experience, she'd be a fantastic addition to the firm. Tasha Smith-Bernard—George's long-time executive assistant—had retired, thus making the position available. Elizabeth was happy she was awarded the job.

When Jennifer and Elizabeth were children, they had an intense sibling rivalry, and the rivalry had continued over the years, until Jennifer's death. It had always remained a mystery even to Elizabeth and Jennifer's parents because they couldn't get along. Yet, Elizabeth and Jennifer had ideas about the reason for their never-ending rivalry, and often argued about it.

Three days after Elizabeth was hired by Butler, Sterling & Burgess, the sisters unexpectedly bumped into each other. Never did they imagine they would have a reunion with each other after many years, and that it would occur at Butler, Sterling & Burgess on a bright and sunny Windy City morning. Despite their long separation, though, they exchanged unpleasant words, fueled by their horrid contempt for each other, which remained all these years.

"Long time no see, Jennifer," Elizabeth said, stunned to see her sister as she entered the managing partner's office.

"Why are you here, Elizabeth?" Jennifer frowned.

"I should ask you that," Elizabeth said as she picked up a file off George's desk.

"George Hawkins, the managing partner of this firm, happens to be my husband."

"I knew he had a wife, but I didn't know you were the ugly bitch he'd married. I just started working here. I didn't see any pictures of you on his desk. If I had, I would have immediately resigned."

"I wished you had," Jennifer replied, rolling her eyes. "Anyway, I'm here to drop this off," Jennifer added as she opened the bag in her hand, just next to her purse, and pulled out the picture of herself, George, and their three children inside a new picture frame. "George accidentally broke our previous family picture frame on his desk. Tasha, his former executive assistant, asked me for another family picture and frame before she retired. I'm just getting around to dropping this off."

"I have to look at your disgusting face every time I have to go into George's office and see that family photo?"

"Go to hell, Elizabeth!" exclaimed Jennifer. "You still haven't changed. You and your nasty attitude tell me you're still jealous of me . . . always have been and always will be."

"Me jealous of you?" Elizabeth said as she broke into laughter. "It's the other way around, bitch!"

"I've never been jealous of you," replied Jennifer. "There's nothing you have that I want."

"You wish you were a blonde like me, don't you?" replied Elizabeth. "You wish you had my nice figure and great looks, right?"

"Brunettes have just as much fun as any blonde. Besides, even after I've given birth to twins, my body looks just as good as yours."

"Ever since we were children, you've always done everything you could to make me jealous of you when it's always been the other way around."

"Yeah, right," exclaimed Jennifer. "What, just because you were born five minutes before me, I'm supposed to show you respect as my older sister?"

"Look, I have work to do! Arguing with you isn't putting a dollar bill into my bank account."

"Yeah, well, I too have work to do," replied Jennifer. "I'm the managing partner at Smith & Harpers, and I'd feel more fulfilled being back in my office than standing here wasting my time with you. You're not on my level, and you never will be."

"When will you ever stop being a bitch, Jennifer?"

"That's the last time you'll ever call me that nasty name!" exclaimed Jennifer. "Don't you ever call me that filthy name again or any other disgusting name or I'll see that you are fired!"

"Threatening me, Mrs. Hawkins?"

"No," Jennifer replied. "It's a promise. Try me, and your days at this firm are numbered!"

As Jennifer exited her husband's office, Elizabeth stood watching her sister. Hearing Jennifer tell her she'd have her fired if she crossed her again by calling her an ugly name or two only made Elizabeth hate her sister even more.

Elizabeth had always felt she was in her sister's shadow. Elizabeth was the high school cheerleader, while Jennifer was the bookworm. Jennifer had always been the object of guys' attention, attention Elizabeth wished she had.

I'm sick and tired of you, Jennifer. You always felt you had the upper hand on me. You always thought you were my boss. Even today, you still feel that way. I'm no longer having any of it. I'm tired of feeling like I'm subservient to you, Jennifer. I'll teach you a lesson, one you'll never forget.

Four months later, that lesson came. Jennifer arrived late at the Butler, Sterling & Burgess office on the night of her sudden death to see her husband, but George wasn't there. It was the night Jennifer and Lawrence had planned to meet and reveal to their respective spouses their desire to get a divorce from them.

Before meeting Lawrence downtown at their favorite restaurant, Jennifer wants to meet with George and tell him she wants to end their marriage and run away with Lawrence. Jennifer was tired of holding on to her secret and wanted to be free.

Yet, when Jennifer arrived at the firm, George had already left to have drinks with a few of the law firm's partners. Butler, Sterling & Burgess was empty, except for a handful of staff. Jennifer found Elizabeth in George's office, listening to the dictations George had done earlier in the day. The dictation machine Elizabeth typically used in her office hadn't been working for days, and she was waiting for a new one to arrive, so she used the one in George's office.

"Well, well, well, the brunette bitch is back!" exclaimed Elizabeth as she broke into laughter. "What brings you here tonight, you ugly ass bitch?"

"I told you months ago never to call me that name or any other demeaning name!"

"Like I give a damn!" Elizabeth said as she rose from the desk and approached her sister. "I wished Mom and Dad gave you up for adoption when you were born. I never understood why our parents didn't have more children besides us. I never wanted you to be my sister."

"You were never a walk in the park yourself, Elizabeth. Maybe if you spent more time learning to love me instead of being so jealous of me, you would have found out what a great sister I could have been to you."

"Go to hell!" Elizabeth said as she forcefully slapped her sister, knocking her to the floor. Elizabeth then kicked and punched Jennifer in the head.

"Stop it . . . just stop it! I feel hurt, Elizabeth! Stop it!" Jennifer loudly exclaimed, hoping someone would hear her. But no one did.

Jennifer fought back as hard as she could, but Elizabeth's firm grip around Jennifer's neck prompted Jennifer to feel lightheaded as she tried to catch her breath. The aggressive alteration triggered Jennifer's asthma attack. Jennifer's collapsed body remained on the floor as she struggled to catch her breath.

Instead of dialing 911 to get medical assistance for her sister, Elizabeth left her on the floor, gasping for breath. Elizabeth knew her sister Jennifer suffered from asthma ever since they were children. Jennifer had always had it from the day she was born, but Elizabeth was spared. Over the years, Jennifer's medical condition worsened despite receiving medical treatment.

During their childhood fights, Elizabeth often retaliated against her sister by doing whatever she could to trigger Jennifer's asthma attacks. Elizabeth had done the same thing in this instance. Sadly, it led to Jennifer's death.

Grabbing her purse and briefcase, Elizabeth quickly left the office, trying hard to conceal her horrific deed. Racing into the underground parking lot, Elizabeth got into her car and hurried down the road, silently thinking of her alibi as she rushed home.

Elizabeth knew she'd deny any involvement in Jennifer's death if ever she were asked. However, when questioned by the authorities the next day at work, Elizabeth vehemently declared George must have returned to the office and committed the crime after she'd gone home from work last night.

When the authorities further probed why she was certain George had killed his wife, Elizabeth told them three weeks ago, she had gone out to buy lunch for George, something she'd often done as his assistant. When she entered his office to hand him his meal, George was deeply engrossed in a newspaper article on a high school friend with whom he'd lost contact.

George last saw his male comrade at their high school graduation. The two men attended different universities: George headed to Princeton, and his friend Albert Stevens was accepted to Yale. The two young men thus parted ways and wished each other the best.

It stunned George when he read the article and saw Albert Stevens—a wealthy Wall St. investment banker—had been found guilty of having his wife kidnapped and murdered so he could collect twenty-five million dollars from a life insurance policy.

As Elizabeth stood in George's office and heard George talk about the brotherly bond he once shared with Albert Stevens and how George had regretted losing touch with Albert, it surprised her when George told her he should increase his family's life insurance policy as well to 25 million dollars to ensure his wife Jennifer and their children Anna, Abigail, and Jonathan would be more than sufficiently taken care of in case of his death.

George made this declaration innocently, not out of any intention to engage in any illegal activity against his wife and children. Elizabeth knew this. She could tell from George's words and tone that it had come from the heart of a caring and concerned husband and father.

Elizabeth was surprised by George's comment because seeing a man so in love with his wife and doting on his children was refreshing. Elizabeth had always wanted that for herself. She had always wanted to find a man who loved her as much as George loved Jennifer.

Elizabeth had always wished to have a husband, children, and a white picket fence home. If she couldn't have all of those, however, she was willing to settle for having a good husband. Yet, she'd never married, nor had she ever had children.

The lack of a good husband, a child or even children, and a white picket fence to enshrine such a dream often caused Elizabeth to feel sad, but she kept hoping that one day, someday, things would turn around and she could have her happily ever after, just as Jennifer had hers.

Clearing her throat as the police continued their interrogation while seated in Elizabeth's office, Elizabeth chose to highlight George's comment about increasing his family's life insurance policy amount, twisting his innocent intentions, and using his words to implicate him and to save herself. While engaging with the police, Elizabeth tries to paint George as a man driven by the love of money. With feigned tears in her eyes, she went as far as saying she had felt it a bit strange to hear George focus on the financial aspect of the news story when a woman had just lost her life due to her husband's felonious plot.

In truth, when George and Elizabeth discussed the unbelievable crime perpetrated by George's old friend Albert Stevens, George expressed great disdain for what his friend had done, wondering aloud how a husband and father could commit such an evil deed and destroy his own family. George was appalled at what his friend had done.

In the same conversation between Elizabeth and George, George's eyes welled with tears when he shared how devastated he'd be if anything ever happened to his wife, Jennifer, and their three children, Anna, Abigail, and Jonathan. Grabbing a tissue from the box of Kleenex on his desk to wipe his flowing tears, George said, "My heart would be broken into a trillion pieces if I ever lost Jennifer and if something horrific befell our dear children."

Elizabeth never shared these sentiments of George with the authorities when she was being interrogated. She never mentioned George's tears when he thought of any harm that may occur to his wife and children. She never shared how saddened and crushed George would be if Jennifer, Anna, Abigail, and Jonathan were no longer in his life.

"I'm stunned to hear you get so choked up like this," Elizabeth said, feeling uneasy, touched by George's affection for his family.

Still unaware that the woman he was talking to was his sister-in-law, George replied, "I would never do the horrendous deed my high school friend did to his wife. I've never lifted my hands to my wife, our children, or anyone else to do any harm. That's not the kind of man I am. Never have been and never will be. How pathetic Albert Stevens was to have allowed his greed to destroy his wife and his life."

"Did the article say if they had children?" Elizabeth asked.

"They had two sons," George answered as he wiped the remnants of his tears. "Now, those young men are without their mother. What a tragedy! What a damn tragedy indeed!"

Those were the parts of the conversation Elizabeth intentionally left out when the authorities interrogated her about the death of her sister, Jennifer. Elizabeth only highlighted the comment George had made about his friend's 25-million-dollar life insurance policy and George's plans to increase his own family's life insurance policy to twenty-five million dollars as well. Elizabeth never mentions George's disgust for his friend Albert Stevens and George's outrage over what Albert Stevens did to satisfy his lust for money.

Even as Elizabeth saw the tears that flowed from George's eyes as he relayed how brokenhearted he'd be if anything bad ever happened to his family, she chose to think only of herself and how to get back at her sister Jennifer for all the times she, Elizabeth, wished she'd had the attention, adoration, compliments, and love Jennifer had received. No longer wanting to heal the feelings of envy and jealousy gnawing at her heart, Elizabeth took a more sinister path: ending the life of her sister and now accusing George of a crime she had viciously committed.

EIGHT

Trying as best she could to cover up her murderous act, Elizabeth set about establishing an ally for her crime. She didn't know where or how to obtain one, but she stayed open to the idea.

Among all the people at Jennifer's funeral, Lawrence seemed to have been the one most visibly shaken by Jennifer's death. Sitting directly behind Lawrence at the solemn farewell, Elizabeth took note of Lawrence's grief. *Was there something here? Why is he crying so much?* Elizabeth pondered as she watched Lawrence pour out his anguishing grief, weeping profusely and uncontrollably like a child.

Elizabeth couldn't understand why Lawrence appeared so heartbroken over Jennifer's death but was determined to find out why. Elizabeth sensed she could use the reason behind Lawrence's grief for her cover-up. Lawrence and others walked to the podium during Jennifer's funeral to share their condolences. The touching words deeply moved Abigail, Anna, Jonathan, and the extended family members, sometimes to tears.

After the poignant funeral, while in the funeral home's parking lot, Elizabeth learned Lawrence had parked next to her car. Elizabeth watched Lawrence retrieve his car keys and stride toward his car. With marks of tears still in his eyes, Elizabeth walked over to him and greeted him, seeking to console him as she gathered information.

"That was a very stirring funeral," Elizabeth said before Lawrence.

With a long sigh, slightly startled, Lawrence said, "Yeah, it was."

"I sat behind you inside the funeral. I noticed you were very sorrowful during the service," said Elizabeth as she fished for information. "I'm sorry," she added, "My name is Elizabeth Jones. I work at Butler, Sterling & Burgess. I started working there a brief time ago. I work for the managing partner,

George Hawkins. The law firm is so large, but I've seen you occasionally in the hallways and a few times when you came to George's office for a meeting."

"I've seen you around the firm, too," replied Lawrence. "There were at least six or seven temporary executive assistants before you started. They came on board when George's long-time executive assistant retired. I wasn't sure you were a temp, just like the others."

"I'm the full-time replacement," replied Elizabeth. "I think your name's Lawrence Wilcox."

"It is." Lawrence smiled as he tried to maintain his saddened composure. "I've been with the law firm for two years."

"Did you know Jennifer?" Elizabeth asked.

"Only as George's wife," Lawrence replied, trying to hide his secret. "I've heard she was a brilliant attorney."

"I've heard that too," replied Elizabeth as she studied his handsome but grief-stricken face. "I know she was the managing partner at Smith & Harpers."

"She will be missed," Lawrence said as he fought back his tears.

"I'm sure."

"I have to make a run."

"Oh, you're not going to the gravesite?" asked Elizabeth with a frown, still looking for clues.

"No. I, um, um." He suddenly paused. "No." Lawrence sighed.

"Maybe we can chat some more at the repast if you're coming."

"Sure. I'll be there."

"Do you mind if I hug you? You seemed so sad."

"Jennifer was a good woman. She didn't deserve to be taken away like this."

Elizabeth quickly embraced Lawrence without waiting for his response. His strong arms caused Elizabeth to remember a man hadn't touched her since her last boyfriend eight months ago.

Pulling back from the hug, Elizabeth noticed the wedding ring on Lawrence's finger. *If Lawrence hugged this good, I'd bet he's dynamite in bed. His wife must be a sexually satisfied woman.*

"I see you're married. Your wife didn't want to attend the funeral with you?"

"She's out of town, visiting her older sister Dorothy in Cleveland, Ohio. Dorothy and her husband have a newborn," George said as he wiped his tears. "My wife Samantha went there to help. Dorothy and Samantha are close."

"It's always nice when sisters are best buddies," replied Elizabeth, not believing her words.

"Did you know Jennifer?" Lawrence asked with a curious stare.

"Um, she was married to George, so out of respect, I came to support my boss—oh, excuse me, our boss," Elizabeth said, not answering the question.

"Nice talking to you, Elizabeth. See you around."

"I'll save you a seat next to me at the repast."

"Much appreciated."

The funeral was held at Stovsky's Funeral Home, one of Chicago's most noted funeral homes. George was not allowed to attend as he was incarcerated. Still, Abigail, Anna, and Jonathan were there, along with extended family members, colleagues from George and Jennifer's law firms, and family friends.

The funeral was held at a large venue. Still, Abigail, Anna, and Jonathan had the repast at an even larger venue that could accommodate the huge crowd that attended: the ballroom of a popular downtown hotel.

Lawrence enjoyed Elizabeth's kindness during the repast and cherished her comforting words. After gorging their meals, Elizabeth and Lawrence exited the venue and walked toward their respective cars. To their surprise, they'd parked beside each other in the hotel's parking lot.

During Jennifer's funeral, Lawrence sat through the service and reflected on his sexual affair with Jennifer. Lawrence had dated women before his marriage, but his time with Jennifer was priceless. Every time they met, their clothes caressed the floor as their lips, hands, legs, and genitalia met.

When Lawrence started his affair with Jennifer, he had guilty pangs for cheating on his wife. Lawrence and Samantha had been married only for six months when he began working at the law firm.

Lawrence and Samantha were in marital bliss, or at least that's what they both thought before Jennifer entered the picture. Having met during their last year in law school---Samantha at Columbia University Law School and Lawrence at NYU Law School—Lawrence and Samantha quickly grew to like each other.

Both avid sports fans and enthusiastic world travelers, Lawrence and Samantha's casual meeting at a mutual friend's birthday party turned into romance. After exchanging nuptials at Samantha's New York City Lutheran church, Lawrence surprised Samantha with a two-week cruise to the Mediterranean for their honeymoon.

To Lawrence and Samantha's surprise, while on their luxurious honeymoon cruise, they met an A-list Hollywood star onboard the cruiser whom Samantha was a huge fan of and whom some had said Samantha bore a resemblance: Jennifer Garner. Meeting a huge celebrity and marrying the man of her dreams were beyond Samantha's wildest dreams. Samantha felt she'd won a million-dollar lottery twice in one day. She was so excited.

Lawrence often reflected on his wedding day during his affair with Jennifer. Standing in the sanctuary of St. John's Lutheran Church in Manhattan, New York, surrounded by hundreds of family members and friends and Samantha standing before him, Lawrence pledged his undying love to Samantha, promising to forsake all others. Since becoming involved with Jennifer, Lawrence often asked himself if he truly meant those words he uttered when he wed Samantha. Gradually, his "I do" had transformed into "I don't."

As Lawrence tried to listen to the funeral participants share their heartfelt words for and about Jennifer, Lawrence promised himself his romance with Jennifer would be the only time he'd ever cheat on his wife. Knowing the pain of losing Jennifer, Lawrence wanted to do all he could to permanently close the door on any more extramarital affairs . . . for good.

NINE

A week after Jennifer's funeral, Elizabeth calculatingly reached out to Lawrence after noticing he had been away from work. Elizabeth wanted to see how Lawrence was holding up after Jennifer's death. She left a voicemail on Lawrence's work phone, greeting and wishing him a wonderful day. She looked forward to Lawrence retrieving the message before or after he returned to work. Either way, Elizabeth was anxious to see him.

When Elizabeth phoned Lawrence and left a voicemail on his work phone, she was unaware of Lawrence's affair with Jennifer, but all that changed on the day Lawrence returned to work. Three days after Elizabeth left the voicemail, Lawrence returned to the office and stayed late on his first day back.

Lawrence took the elevator to the firm's second-floor cafeteria for a late dinner. With so much on his mind, and especially Jennifer's death, Lawrence accidentally left his cell phone on a table in the cafeteria after retrieving his meal. Minutes after Lawrence exited the cafeteria without his cell phone, Elizabeth entered and chose her meal before casually picking the table where Lawrence had accidentally left his phone.

Elizabeth scrolled through the cell phone to find out who its owner was so she could return it to him or her, but she was stunned to discover the cell phone belonged to Lawrence. She saw texts upon texts of hot and sultry exchanges between her sister Jennifer and Lawrence, and naked pictures and naked videos of the two. Elizabeth was shocked. She didn't know and did not suspect anything improper happened between Lawrence and Jennifer. Why, Elizabeth had no idea Jennifer and Lawrence were an item.

How were they able to keep this a secret? Jennifer and Lawrence had sex? My, this is juicy!

From the day Elizabeth started working at the law firm, she had seen Lawrence in the hallways, cafeteria, and the other associates' and partners' offices, including George's. She was impressed with Lawrence's tall, muscular frame and green eyes. His frame made her think of the handsome tennis players she'd often seen on TV. The wedding ring on his finger let everyone know he was off limits romantically, so Elizabeth never came on to him even though she had wanted to.

Learning Lawrence and her sister Jennifer had been getting it on made Elizabeth regret she had not sampled, sucked, licked, and sexed the package inside Lawrence's pants. Elizabeth placed the cell phone inside her purse and quickly left the cafeteria. She immediately put Lawrence's cell phone inside her desk drawer when she reached her office. She then locked the drawer.

When she got to work the next day, Elizabeth emailed Lawrence and told him to retrieve his cell phone from her. After arriving at the office, Lawrence anxiously rushed to Elizabeth's room.

"Come in!" exclaimed Elizabeth, hearing a knock at her office door and suspecting it was Lawrence.

"Is this a suitable time?" Lawrence asked with a worried look as he rushed into the room. "I got your voicemail. I came to get my phone." Lawrence quickly closed the door behind him.

"Hello, Lawrence," Elizabeth replied with a smile, sexily playing with the strands of her hair. "Now's a great time, actually, Lawrence. I'm glad you're here."

During her drive to work, Elizabeth sat in her car and thought of ways to use her sister's steamy affair with Lawrence for her benefit. *You've always acted as though you were better than me, Jennifer, but the text messages and naked pictures, and nude videos I saw of you and Lawrence in Lawrence's phone prove you're nothing but a whore!*

I've never been married and had no children, but if I vowed to be faithful to my husband, I'd do it and be an excellent role model for my children.

As for you, Lawrence Wilcox, here you are cheating on your wife. I wonder how good you are in bed. I don't condone married people cheating on their spouses, but in this situation, I'll set aside my morals. I'll have my way with you, Attorney Lawrence Wilcox.

Had Lawrence been getting it on with any other woman and not my sister, I wouldn't care. Now that I know Lawrence had an affair with my sister, however, how could I turn my back on the opportunity to knock Jennifer off her pedestal . . . even after her death? I want to be the woman Lawrence desires. I want to be the woman Lawrence falls madly in love with now. I want our bond to make Lawrence forget all about Jennifer.

When Jennifer and I were still children, it made me angry when everyone praised Jennifer for her beauty and smarts and for how well she could dance ballet, play the piano, and do gymnastics. I was as beautiful and bright as Jennifer. . . I also played the piano, did gymnastics, and danced ballet, so why did people, including our parents, constantly praise Jennifer and ignore me?

"May I have my phone?" Lawrence asked as Elizabeth snapped out of her daydreaming.

"Oh, yes, the phone . . . your phone," Elizabeth replied as she stood and retrieved the drawer's keys from her purse. She unlocked the drawer and handed him his cell phone, placing her keys on her desk before returning to her seat.

"Thanks," Lawrence said as he stood at Elizabeth's desk with a look of relief. He had not realized his phone had been missing until Elizabeth contacted him.

"You need to do a better job of securing your phone, Lawrence. You didn't even put your phone on lock, nor did you use a passcode. You don't want anyone to know that . . ."

"I know what you're about to say, and . . ."

"What was I about to say?" interjected Elizabeth with a mischievous smile.

"I don't have to tell you. You probably . . ."

"Probably what?" Elizabeth interjected, signaling him to take a seat. He obliged.

"Look, um, um . . ."

"Why don't we meet after work and talk about this?" Elizabeth replied, pretending not to know what Lawrence was referring to.

"I'd appreciate it if you didn't share anything you saw on my phone with anyone. Women like to scroll through a man's phone, and . . ."

"Is there something you didn't want me to see, Lawrence?" Elizabeth interjected.

"I plead the fifth."

Elizabeth grabbed a blank piece of paper and an ink pen from her desk and wrote down her address and phone number. She handed the paper to Lawrence and said, "This is my address and cell phone number, too. Come over for dinner tonight at 7:30 p.m. We can discuss what you thought I saw on your phone tonight."

"Tonight's not good. My wife and I are . . ."

"I don't care what you and your wife had planned for tonight, Attorney Wilcox. Whatever it is, I suggest you cancel it and come to my place if you know what's best for you."

"And if I don't?"

With a smirk, Elizabeth said, "You'll miss my delicious cooking, for one. Two, you'll miss dessert. Three, I might have to tell George you and his deceased wife had been . . ."

"You wouldn't dare!" interrupted Lawrence, abruptly standing.

"If I open my front door at 7:30 p.m. and I don't see you, then you'll give me no other option but to tell our boss you were screwing his wife, Jennifer."

"I'll lose everything if you do that, Elizabeth!"

"Not if you do what I said."

"Fine," Lawrence replied with a sigh. "I'll be there," he replied, rushing out of her office with a stern look.

TEN

Lawrence parked his car outside Elizabeth's house and walked up the flower-covered pathway to the front of her door. He paused, glanced at his watch, and noted the time: 7:28 p.m. Lawrence and his wife Samantha had plans to have dinner at their favorite Italian restaurant tonight, but Lawrence called Samantha at her office and lied to her, telling her he had to work late. He then assured Samantha that he'd make it up to her.

Lawrence stood in front of Elizabeth's door. Before Lawrence touched Elizabeth's doorbell, he thought about turning around, getting back into his car, and telling Samantha about his affair with Jennifer.

But I can't. I have too much to lose. What if Samantha divorced me? What if the law firm found out and I lost my job? What if all the law firms in town banned me if they found out I was having an affair with the wife of the managing partner of the law firm? What if everyone started thinking I had something to do with Jennifer's death? What if everyone told me I killed Jennifer?

Lawrence stoically stood at Elizabeth's front door, lost to his thoughts. Suddenly, without pressing the doorbell, the front door opened. Elizabeth stood at the doorway with a broad smile and wore a house coat. "Come in, Lawrence."

Lawrence followed her lead and walked behind her as she entered the house. Lawrence then closed the door behind him. Turning his head, he saw Elizabeth disrobe, wearing nothing underneath.

"Elizabeth . . . listen . . . please listen . . ."

"Cell phone, Lawrence. Cell phone." Elizabeth grinned and winked.

"What are you saying?" Lawrence asked. "What's your point?"

"You already know the answers to both questions, my dear," replied Elizabeth. "Do as I say, and you won't have any problem. I want you to make love to me tonight." Elizabeth smiled. "But first, I need to tell you something."

"What's that?" asked Lawrence.

"That woman you were screwing, Jennifer? She was my fraternal twin sister."

"Jennifer . . . George Hawkins' wife, was your fraternal twin sister?" Lawrence asked, with shock written all over his face.

"Yes," replied Elizabeth, nodding her head while chuckling. "No one at the law firm knew that. Jennifer and I rarely told anyone. Of course, when we were still children and adolescents, many knew. Still, I didn't like to talk about it, and I know Jennifer didn't like to discuss it either, especially since we didn't like each other," added Elizabeth, shrugging her shoulders. "I supposed it didn't matter that Jennifer and I didn't discuss being sisters since she and I had never been close."

"Elizabeth," Lawrence replied, "I don't know how I feel about sexing two sisters. I know a lot of men have that as a sexual fantasy . . . having sex with two sisters . . . but it's never been mine! I didn't even know you and Jennifer were related! You don't look alike at all!"

Elizabeth ignored his remarks and said, "You dated my sister Jennifer for two years. I read that in one of your text messages to Jennifer."

"And?"

"How long do you think you and I should date?"

"Elizabeth, listen . . ."

"Lawrence," Elizabeth said as she gently led him into her living room naked. "Do you want to eat me first, or do you want first to have the dinner I prepared? I prepared lasagna."

Lawrence, still stunned by her nakedness, said, "Elizabeth, listen, please." He saw Elizabeth walk over to the mirror just behind her and wondered what she was doing.

"I left early from work today to get home and prepare our meals for tonight," Elizabeth said. "While cooking and baking in the kitchen, I watched TV. An old movie came on," said Elizabeth, "starring Michelle Pfeiffer and Robert Redford. The movie was "Up Close and Personal." It was so sexy and sweet," Elizabeth said as she walked toward Lawrence.

"And you're telling me this because?"

Standing before Lawrence, gently touching his face, Elizabeth said, "People have told me I looked like a blonde Michelle Pfeiffer. She's beautiful, so I'll take that as a compliment. Do you think I'm beautiful, Lawrence?"

"I don't know who Michelle Pfeiffer is, but yes, you're a beautiful woman."

"And you're a handsome man," Elizabeth said as she kissed Lawrence on the neck.

"Elizabeth . . . Elizabeth," Lawrence said, trying to resist. "I swore to myself I would no longer cheat on my wife."

"You swore too soon."

"But I . . ."

"I promise you I won't hurt you. I'm easy to please in bed," replied Elizabeth. "Why don't we do this," Elizabeth said as she embraced him, pulling his arms around her. "Let's eat dinner first and then go to one of my three bedrooms upstairs."

"Why am I here?"

"Don't play dumb, baby," Elizabeth said, laughing. "I fixed a nice homemade apple pie and a peach cobbler. You can have either of those after dinner or before we have sex."

"I feel like a fool," replied Lawrence as he broke into a long sigh. "I screwed one sister, and now . . ."

"You get me," interjected Elizabeth. "You saved the best for last, honey," Elizabeth said as she leaned in and gave him an enthusiastic kiss, feeling him surrendering to her touch.

ELEVEN

Lawrence and Elizabeth's affair was now moving into its fifth month. Elizabeth was enjoying her time with Lawrence, especially the sexual leverage she had over him.

The sex was enthusiastic and far from boring, with encounters at Elizabeth's house, in each other's cars, at hotels, motels, and occasionally in the restroom stalls at work, along with stalls in restaurants, gasoline stations, bookstores, libraries, department stores, and even grocery stores. Whenever Lawrence tried to turn down Elizabeth's sexual allurements, Elizabeth mentioned his cell phone, reminding him she'd expose his affair with Jennifer if he ever refused her.

Unknown to Lawrence, of course, just before Elizabeth locked his cell phone in her office drawer—on the night before Elizabeth notified Lawrence, she'd found his cell phone in the firm's cafeteria, Elizabeth stayed late at work and audio taped on a small tape recorder she'd kept at her desk sexy texts she'd read on Lawrence's cell phone between him and Jennifer. Wanting to have weaponry to her advantage, Elizabeth couldn't resist using her cell phone to snap their naked photos and record segments of their naked videos onto her cell phone.

Lawrence would attempt to delete the sexy texts, naked photos, and naked videos, so Elizabeth told herself that she did what she could to savor her sexual blackmail by recording their lustful deeds. To ensure no one would get hold of the tape recorder, Elizabeth took it home and locked it inside the safe at the back of her bedroom closet. Elizabeth didn't tell Lawrence she had done this. She kept it a secret, planning to reveal it to Lawrence only if she needed additional ammunition to control him further.

Pausing from kissing him, Elizabeth said, "The maple syrup on your tongue tastes so good."

"I ordered breakfast for you, Elizabeth," Lawrence said as he and Elizabeth relaxed in a hotel suite. "I put your breakfast in the refrigerator in the other room while you were sleeping. I didn't want to disturb you when the food arrived, so I left it in the refrigerator so you could heat it in the microwave when you woke up."

Elizabeth leaned forward, stood, and walked toward the adjoining room to retrieve her food. Before she could get there, though, she turned and kissed Lawrence on the cheek, wanting to feel his skin against her face. "Thanks for the food, baby. I appreciate that," she added. "What did you think of last night?"

"And early this morning, too?" Lawrence laughed as he walked across the room to sample his near-empty food plate before returning to the bed. "In one word . . . damn!"

"What do you mean by that?" Elizabeth replied, laughing.

"I love your sex drive, Elizabeth. You know what you want when it comes to sex, and you have no problem letting me know. I love that about you."

"Closed mouths don't get fed. It would help if you asked for what you want. You got to go for what you want, too, in and out of bed," replied Elizabeth.

"And you certainly don't mind asking . . . and even taking," Lawrence replied. "I liked the way you grabbed my member and feasted on it," he said, seeing her smile.

"The way I gave you oral sex?"

"Yeah," he answered with a grin. "You gave my dick a workout with that pretty mouth of yours."

"I wanted you to be satisfied just as much as I was, Lawrence."

"Mission accomplished, baby," he replied as they both laughed.

"I also loved the way you made me so wet."

"Anytime, baby," Lawrence said with a wink and a smile. "Anytime for you."

Starting to feel hunger pangs, Elizabeth resumed her walk into the other room, got her plate of food, and put it inside the microwave for a few minutes. She then retrieved her plate from the microwave and then turned to retrieve the fork to her right. Elizabeth sampled the potatoes, eggs, sausages, and pancakes and adored their delicious taste.

Staring at Elizabeth as he leaned back in bed, Lawrence smiled and said, "The food's good, huh?"

"Excellent," replied Elizabeth as she returned to bed carrying her food plate.

"I knew with all the sex we were having, we'd end up very hungry. All that sexing can wear out a person."

"Speak for yourself. I could go for another round or two or three or four more," Elizabeth said, laughing as she sat her food plate on the nightstand beside her.

"What time are you checking out?" Lawrence asked.

"I asked for a late check-out," Elizabeth answered. "I should be gone by 2 p.m."

"You have plans for the day?" he asked.

"Sleeping and swimming a few laps in my outdoor pool when I get home."

"Sounds good," Lawrence replied. "I need to go to the firm's Los Angeles office next week, and then I'll be off to our office in Cleveland the following week before I get back home to Chicago . . ."

"Sexing me again," Elizabeth interjected. "I can't get enough of your body."

"Good," replied Lawrence, seeing Elizabeth lift her fork and partake of her breakfast.

"What do you have planned for today, Lawrence?"

"Just chilling at home with my wife Samantha. We might watch a movie."

"Sounds like a wonderful way to spend a Sunday."

"I wish I had you by my side all day. I like you, Elizabeth."

Elizabeth smiled as she bit into her food, enjoying his compliments. Just as Elizabeth was about to take another bite of her food, she heard her cell phone ring. "I'd better see who that is, although I already know."

"Who?"

"My lawn technician. I almost forgot. He's supposed to come to my house today and tidy my front and back yards," Elizabeth said, walking across the room and retrieving her cell phone from her purse, checking the caller ID, and noting that it was indeed her lawn technician.

Lawrence watched Elizabeth talking on her cell phone, seated in a nearby chair. He walked over to her, still yearning for her touch and needing to feel her skin against his again. He knelt in front of Elizabeth's naked body and kissed her thighs. He then slowly opened her legs and brushed his tongue against her clitoris and vagina, moving in and out and up and down.

Elizabeth tried to push him away but slowly succumbed to his advances. Her wish to enjoy Lawrence's naked body yet again won over her need to talk to her lawn technician. "Donald, I . . . I'll call you back later," Elizabeth said as she clicked off her cell phone.

"You cut off your conversation with your lawn technician?" Lawrence asked, pleased he'd gotten Elizabeth off the phone.

"You already know the answer to that, Lawrence," Elizabeth said, sliding down a little further in her chair to enjoy the oral stimulation he was giving her.

"You feel good, huh?"

"Oh, yes," Elizabeth replied as she closed her eyes, resting her cell phone on the table to her right.

"I have an idea."

"What's that?" Elizabeth said as she opened her eyes, taking in the moment.

"Something sexual I want us to try."

"Okay," she replied with a frown. "We've already tried several positions. What, you want to ride me from the back again . . . you know, doggy style?"

"Not this time, baby," Lawrence replied with a playful smile. "Why don't we take a shower together? One of my fantasies is we'd make love in the shower. We've never done that before."

"Funny, that's also one of my fantasies."

"What are we waiting for?"

"Let's get wet!"

"Not quite," Lawrence said as he stood.

"What do you have in mind?" Elizabeth said, seeing Lawrence walk over to his pile of clothes and retrieve his belt and silk tie.

Holding his belt and necktie as he walked over to her, Lawrence said, "While you're in the shower, I want to wrap this tie around your eyes."

"Okay."

"As for the belt," Lawrence said as he watched her face, weighing her interest in what he was saying, "I want to put it around your neck while I'm inside you."

"You want to be extra freaky?" Elizabeth asked, breaking into laughter. "I've never made love with a belt around my neck or a necktie around my eyes, but there's a first time for everything, right?"

"You told me weeks ago that the other Elizabeth likes to come out and play on rare occasions."

"Now's my time," Elizabeth replied with a wink. "Let's play, baby."

Elizabeth stood and walked toward the bathroom. Lawrence followed with his belt and necktie in his hands. Upon entering the bathroom, he saw that Elizabeth had gotten into the shower and had already started to lather her body with soap and water.

With Elizabeth's back facing him, Lawrence stared at her with intense longing as his penis grew hard. He felt he could make love to her without delay, but he did not want to pass up the chance to use his belt and necktie for a little sexual fun.

Turning around to look at Lawrence and see him standing in the bathroom doorway with the belt and necktie in his hands, Elizabeth asked, "Are you getting in? What are you waiting for?"

"One second, Elizabeth. I'll be right there."

"All right, but don't keep me waiting," Elizabeth said as she turned her back and continued applying more soap and water to her body, relishing the lather.

Making sure she wasn't looking his way, Lawrence rushed into the other room and grabbed his cell phone to take pictures of her. With her back still facing him, Lawrence slowly moved toward the bathroom and quietly snapped a few photos of Elizabeth before returning his cell phone to the table.

Lawrence returned to the bathroom carrying both when he retrieved the belt and necktie he had left at the table in the other room when he got his phone.

"Lawrence, are you coming?" hollered Elizabeth. "Hurry up!"

"I'll be right there, Elizabeth!" Lawrence replied.

Seeing his erect penis as he stood in the doorway, Elizabeth said, "Get in here. I'm ready to play, big boy."

"And I'm ready to play with you," Lawrence replied as he stepped into the shower, holding the belt and tie. Gently kissing her lips, Lawrence said, "Close your eyes. Let me tie this necktie over them."

"Not too tight," Elizabeth said as the necktie caressed her face, feeling the tie now cover her eyes.

 "Lift your arms high," he said. She obeyed his instructions, and he slowly attached the belt to her neck. "I won't make it too tight."

"Now what?" Elizabeth asked, trying to resist laughing and feeling silly but turned on, too.

"Just move in closer to me," Lawrence said as he gently kissed her neck and breasts, then slowly moved his penis inside her wet vaginal walls.

Lawrence smiled as he saw the grin on Elizabeth's face, seeing her enjoy the tie around her eyes. He couldn't wait to place the belt around her neck. He was happy she was willing to play this sex game, as he was enjoying it immensely.

What happened when Lawrence and Elizabeth entered the room last night happened again, but this time in the shower. The twitching of their wet bodies and the twisting of their wet backs heightened their excitement. The orgasmic thrusting of their wet bodies went on and on until they both peaked in ecstasy.

TWELVE

A week passed, and Lawrence and Elizabeth met again at the same downtown Chicago hotel where they last met. After a passion-filled night, Elizabeth and Lawrence awakened the following day, ready to order room service for breakfast. Elizabeth turned and smiled at Lawrence, and Lawrence leaned in and kissed her tenderly.

"As terrible as I feel about cheating on my wife, I must admit you certainly know how to satisfy me like no other woman ever has."

"Even my sister Jennifer?"

"To be honest . . . yes," Lawrence replied. "You take the cake, Elizabeth. I love the way you make me feel when . . ."

"We're making love?"

"Yes," he replied, leaning in to kiss her again. "No other woman has ever sucked my penis the way you do. I'm not a religious man, but Elizabeth, I feel like I'm in heaven when your mouth touches my member." He smiled.

"I also loved it when your lips touched my lips, neck, breasts, clitoris, thighs, butt . . . my entire body, Lawrence. You always send me into the height of happiness, baby."

"I want more and more of you," Lawrence said with a chuckle.

Elizabeth winked at him as she thought to herself how confident she felt about her sexual control over Lawrence. Considering this, she believed Lawrence wouldn't expose her secret regarding her sister's death if she revealed it to him.

"I'll keep your secret if you'll keep mine."

"Huh?" replied Lawrence with a frown. "What are you talking about, Elizabeth?"

"There's something I've never told anyone."

"And what's that?" Lawrence said with a frown.

"You won't tell a soul? Promise me."

"I promise," Lawrence said as he looked intensely into her eyes while they both lay naked on the hotel bed.

"I'm responsible for Jennifer's death."

"What do you mean?" asked Lawrence incredulously. "You killed Jennifer?"

"Yes," replied Elizabeth. "It was time for Jennifer to go. I couldn't stand that awful, arrogant bitch!"

"What? How could you! What's wrong with you?" Lawrence said as he immediately got out of the bed, standing before her naked. "You killed your sister?"

"We're not done having sex! Get back in bed, Lawrence!"

"No . . . hell no!" hollered Lawrence. "You're a mean and cruel woman! I should have left you a long time ago! How stupid could I have been?"

"I guess that's what happens when you want your sexual desires always satisfied." Elizabeth laughed and then winked at him seductively.

"No, that's what happens when you don't have the guts to stand up to a despicable woman like you!"

"Come back to bed, Lawrence. Why are you getting so roused up, baby?"

"You just admitted you killed your sister, and you have the nerve to ask me a stupid question like that!" Lawrence said as he hurriedly collected his clothes to quickly exit the room and into the bathroom. "What the hell's wrong with you, woman?"

"Nothing's wrong with me!"

"Have you ever done this before . . . you know, killed anyone?"

"No!" Elizabeth exclaimed, stunned by his question. "What kind of woman do you take me for, Lawrence?"

"I can't believe you killed your sister Jennifer!" Lawrence said, shaking his head.

"Are you leaving?" hollered Elizabeth. "You're leaving me?"

"I should have left you a long time ago. I never should have gotten involved with you to begin with!"

"Calm down, Lawrence. Have you forgotten that you have a lot at stake here? If you leave me, baby, I'll go and tell George you screwed Jennifer! You'll lose everything! Your wife will divorce you; all you'll have is me."

"I'm tired of you blackmailing me, Elizabeth!"

"Get used to it, honey, because I own you, and there's nothing you can do about it."

"We'll see about that!" Lawrence loudly exclaimed. "I loved your sister . . . I loved Jennifer. On the night Jennifer was found dead in the managing partner's office was the very night she and I were . . . were . . ."

"Were what, Lawrence? Elizabeth interjected. "Spit it out, damn it! You and that bitch were going to do what?"

"Never mind," Lawrence replied with a long sigh. "You wouldn't understand. You have such a cruel and mean heart; you wouldn't know love if it kissed you on the lips!"

"Well, I may not know love, but I know great sex," replied Elizabeth as she burst into laughter. "Lawrence, every time you bring me to orgasm, baby, you make me want to pull out a cigarette and smoke . . . and I'm not even a smoker," Elizabeth added, resuming her chuckle. "Your dick works wonders inside of me every time. I want it right now!"

"Savor the orgasms, 'cause today is the last time I will ever have sex with you!"

"Lawrence, calm down," Elizabeth replied as she hurried over to him to caress, hold, and move him back into bed.

Lawrence resisted with a stern look in his eyes. "I want nothing to do with you! You killed the woman I was madly in love with!"

"Jennifer was nothing but a cheating whore! She cheated on her husband with you. She was a piece of crap, Lawrence! You saved the best for last when you got with me, baby! Can't you see that?"

"Say what you want about Jennifer, but I loved that woman!"

"Oh, so you didn't love your wife, Samantha? You weren't in love with your wife?"

"Look," Lawrence replied as he shook his head in frustration. "All I have to say is you and I are done!"

THIRTEEN

Sarah was entirely in the dark regarding what led to Elizabeth and Lawrence's heated exchange in the underground parking lot of the Butler, Sterling & Burgess. It was two weeks ago when Elizabeth and Lawrence had that intense argument in the Chicago hotel room where they had spent the night, and after sleepless nights since then, Lawrence decided today was the day he'd come clean.

Rushing over to Sarah's car with Lawrence behind her, Elizabeth hurriedly pulled a gun from her purse, a weapon she always carried for protection. Upon seeing the gun, Lawrence and Sarah stood speechless, stunned, and in utter disbelief this was happening.

"Sarah Romans!" said Elizabeth.

"She's the receptionist of the law firm," Lawrence said.

"I know," replied Elizabeth. "I bet she heard everything we were just talking about . . . about Jennifer, the sex, and everything else. Did you hear anything about all these, Sarah Romans? Tell me the damn truth!"

"Yeah . . . yes . . . yes, I did," Sarah replied hesitatingly, raising her hands as if to say, "Don't harm me." Staring deeply into Elizabeth's eyes and then turning her head and glancing at Lawrence, Sarah said with mixed bravery and nervousness, "How . . . how . . . how could you do this to the managing partner's wife, Elizabeth? And Attorney Wilcox, I . . . I . . . I . . . can't believe that . . ."

"Shut up, Sarah! Shut your damn mouth now, or I'll shut it permanently!" Elizabeth shouted, glaring at Sarah. Elizabeth turned to look at Lawrence and added, "Sarah knows too much now. That ticks me off!"

Elizabeth pointed the gun at Sarah and Lawrence and motioned them to get into her car. Elizabeth then tossed her car keys to Lawrence, ordering him to enter the driver's seat. Sarah was to get into the passenger seat across from Lawrence.

Elizabeth sat behind Lawrence, with her gun pointed straight ahead. She steadied her hands and prepared herself in case Sarah or Lawrence made a wrong move. Tilting her head to get a side view of their faces, Elizabeth gazed at them with threatening eyes, daring them to escape. In truth, Elizabeth herself wanted to escape. Thus, she ordered Lawrence to take her to Chicago's O'Hare Airport.

Elizabeth had to piece together a new script . . . a new plan of action for the unscripted reality show called Her Life. There was only one place where she could hide: Costa Rica. She thus decided to board a plane to Costa Rica and stay at the modest home she had purchased there several years ago with the money she had saved while serving in the military. *Remaining in Costa Rica for the rest of my life would lessen the chances I would ever get caught for Jennifer's murder*, Elizabeth told herself.

Elizabeth always kept her passport and often used it as her ID. She also had her driver's license and other necessary documents. She had hoped her secret about her involvement in Jennifer's death would never become known, but that hope was dashed when Sarah inadvertently learned about it, forcing Elizabeth to go on the run.

Elizabeth felt safe revealing her secret to Lawrence, believing she could sexually blackmail him to keep his silence. She surmised even if Lawrence declared their hot sex was over, she could continue hiding her crime and blackmailing Lawrence to have more and more sex with her . . . as much as she wanted . . . as often as she liked.

That would not be the case, though. Elizabeth had never imagined her crime and sexual blackmail would come to light . . . certainly not today and certainly not on the day Sarah had planned to quit the firm.

FOURTEEN

Sarah looked at the side mirror occasionally to see what Elizabeth was doing at the back of the car. To her surprise, Elizabeth had moved directly behind her and had picked up her cell phone to respond to texts. While watching Elizabeth, Sarah planned to jump out of the car at the next traffic light and rush to the nearby gas station for help.

From the back of the car, Elizabeth ordered Lawrence to turn on the radio and look for a station reporting the local news. The morning news segment reported the trial of George Hawkins was to start today at 11 a.m., just 3 hours away. Sarah quietly listened to the news and thought to herself it had been some time since the investigation into Jennifer's death started. Sarah had never imagined the day she had planned to resign from the Butler, Sterling & Burgess law firm would be the same day George Hawkins would stand trial for the murder of his wife.

Sarah was outraged the wrong person was standing trial for Jennifer's death. The real culprit was seated behind her. Sarah had to find a way to escape, get to the courthouse, and inform the prosecutor George Hawkins was an innocent man and was not responsible for his wife's death. The chance for her to do this came when she saw Elizabeth suddenly move behind Lawrence again and accidentally dropped her gun on the car floor.

Sarah turned to the left to see if Elizabeth had picked up the gun. Seeing Elizabeth had not and sensing the car was moving at a slower pace, just 20 mph, due to a traffic build-up, Sarah suddenly jumped out of the car and rushed quickly into the gas station's store not too far to her right.

Rushing into the gas station's store, Sarah immediately screamed. "I need the police! Help me now! I need to call the police!" She then turned and locked the front door.

"What are you doing?" the store clerk screamed. "What's going on?"

"I just escaped from a hostage situation!" exclaimed Sarah, trying to catch her breath. "That black car . . . that black Jeep Cherokee . . . the woman inside it held me and the man behind the wheel at gunpoint." Sarah pointed toward the window in the direction of Elizabeth's car. "I need to call the police right now!"

Looking outside the glass door of the gas station's store, Sarah saw Elizabeth's car parked out front. The car door opened, and Elizabeth got out. "She's coming this way! We'd better get down! Where's the phone?" Sarah screamed.

"It's here, on the counter!" the store clerk exclaimed, her eyes filled with horror and panic.

Sarah raced to the phone and dialed 911, quickly relaying their ordeal and location to the operator. She heard Elizabeth banging on and kicking the store's door. The banging and kicking momentarily stopped when Elizabeth heard Lawrence speed off in her jeep.

"Open this damn door, Sarah!" hollered Elizabeth. "Open this door, or I'll shoot!"

Sarah and the store clerk hid behind the counter while waiting for the police. Elizabeth resumed banging and kicking the door, this time with her gun. Within minutes, however, the sirens of police cars blared out front, and Sarah and the store clerk released sighs of relief.

"I said to open this door, Sarah! I know you're in there!" screamed Elizabeth.

The police pulled out their guns and demanded Elizabeth put down her weapon. Elizabeth slowly rested her weapon on the ground and then lifted her empty hands in the air. The police officers apprehended her, and the other officers banged on the door. "Police! Open the door!"

Sarah and the store clerk slowly stood and raced to the door. Sarah then unlocked it.

"Are y'all okay?" the police officers asked the two, showing them their badges.

"Yes," Sarah replied, letting out a long sigh and seeing the store clerk do the same as she ran toward the door and stood beside Sarah.

"Officers, that woman . . . that woman . . . Her name's Elizabeth Jones. She's responsible for the death of her sister, Jennifer Hawkins, but George Hawkins, Jennifer's husband, was blamed for it. His trial starts today at 11 a.m. He's an innocent man. He's standing trial for the murder of his wife, but he didn't do it! Elizabeth Jones did it!"

"How do you know all these?"

"I heard Elizabeth say it nearly 20 minutes ago . . . in the underground parking lot of our law firm . . . Butler, Sterling & Burgess. My name is Sarah Romans. I'm the receptionist of the firm. Elizabeth Jones is the executive assistant of George Hawkins, and the man who was with us in the car but who had sped off is an associate of the same firm. Attorney George Hawkins had been in jail for months, awaiting his trial. He's done nothing wrong. I need to get to the courthouse and tell the judge and the lawyers involved in the case before the trial starts this morning."

The two police officers looked at each other with stunned expressions.

"Elizabeth Jones kidnapped me and our co-worker, Attorney Lawrence Wilcox, at gunpoint. I escaped from her car and ran to this gas station. Our co-worker Attorney Wilcox drove off somewhere."

"Dan, why don't you drive this woman downtown to the courthouse while I get a statement from the clerk?"

FIFTEEN

The clock struck 10:18 a.m., and Sarah and the police officer who had escorted her had just arrived at the courthouse. Quickly walking over to the appropriate courtroom door, Sarah and the police officer spotted a man who was about to enter the courtroom. He looked like an attorney as he was clutching a portfolio. Unknown to Sarah and the police officer, the attorney was from the District Attorney's office.

"Excuse me," the police officer said, addressing the attorney. "Are you by any chance one of the attorneys involved in George Hawkins' criminal case?" The man nodded, and the police officer added, "This young lady needs to share some crucial information with you."

Frowning, the attorney said, "You picked an inconvenient time to talk to me. The trial's about to start."

"Mr. George Hawkins is an innocent man," exclaimed Sarah. "He had nothing to do with his wife's death."

"How do you know this, Miss?" asked the attorney.

"I overheard his sister-in-law say exactly what happened."

"What is the sister-in-law's name?" the attorney asked.

"Elizabeth Jones," Sarah answered.

The trial was delayed for hours as further details were unraveled. At 3 p.m. that afternoon, the local media reported Attorney George Hawkins had been cleared of all the charges leveled against him, and Elizabeth Jones had pleaded guilty to her involvement in her sister's death.

Sarah was finally allowed to leave the courtroom after meeting with the judge, defense attorney, and prosecutor. While walking in the hallway, Sarah spotted Lawrence, who had entered the courthouse minutes ago.

Lawrence told Sarah, "I heard about what happened on the news regarding our boss, George." Lawrence sighed, loosening his tie and running his fingers through his ruffled hair, looking worn. "Looks like you're a hero, Sarah. You're a very courageous woman. You're the reason I came down here."

"What do you mean?" asked Sarah.

"I came to tell the judge everything I know. Your bravery encouraged me to do the right thing," replied Lawrence. "I also told my wife Samantha I was cheating on her with Jennifer and Elizabeth," he added. "Samantha's crushed. She's divorcing me, but at least my conscience is clear." Lawrence sighed and shook his head in frustration. "Maybe I married too young. Maybe I just wasn't mature enough to marry Samantha. I feel terrible. I made a mess of things."

Lawrence walked away, feeling distraught and embarrassed. He paused to ask a police officer for directions to the proper courtroom. Sarah stared at Lawrence, wondering what would become of him.

Suddenly, glancing to her right, Sarah saw her boss, George, hurriedly walking toward her. "Thank you! Thank you!" he screamed to Sarah, quickly embracing her. "This has all been a nightmare," George added, looking weary and worn from his months-long stay in jail.

"You gave me back my freedom!" he hugged her. "You're just the type of worker our law firm needs. A promotion is in order. The executive assistant position is available. I can use your intellect and expertise as my new executive assistant, Sarah."

"Are you offering me the job?" Sarah asked.

"Yes. It's yours!"

"Thank you, sir, but I'll pass."

"Why?" George frowned.

"I love being a receptionist, sir, although I wouldn't mind a raise, a bonus, and certainly more admiration and appreciation for all my work."

"It's all yours, Sarah. Appreciation . . . more money . . . you name it," he said. "I apologize for not honoring all the demanding work you did. That will never happen again. Never!" he emphasized. "Tell me the salary you want, and I'll immediately sign on the dotted line," George said with tears of joy. "You saved my life, Sarah! How can I ever repay you?"

"Thank you, sir," Sarah said as she pulled back from his embrace and looked into his eyes, seeing his sincerity. "I was simply doing my job."

"You went beyond your job, Sarah. Thank you, Sarah!" George said, kneeling before her as if proposing. "I've seen all you've done for the firm, but I've never given you the credit you deserve. You answer the phone, greet the guests and clients, oversee the mail, order the needed supplies, oversee the catering, stay late whenever we need you, type documents, and do so much to make the firm run smoothly . . . And . . . and you gave me back my life, Sarah!" He sobbed like a child.

"It's all in a day's work," replied Sarah, stunned to see her boss on his knees and addressing her in this manner, suddenly standing to embrace her again. "I just wanted to do an excellent job, sir. It's all in a day's work. Truly, it's all in a day's work."

"Lust may have landed me in jail for a crime I didn't commit. Lust and law ferociously battled each other, but lust didn't win. The law won!" George loudly exclaimed, raising his hands in victory. "An innocent man was set free, and I am that innocent man," George exclaimed with joyful tears. "Justice prevailed, and I am here to proclaim my freedom!"

Suddenly, Sarah turned her head and saw Lawrence exiting the courtroom and sitting on a bench near him. With a saddened and troubled look, Lawrence shook his head as he sat in deep thought. Sarah pondered the grand difference between George Hawkins and Lawrence. One is caught in the web of deceit, adultery, and lies, and the other is free from Elizabeth's plot to destroy him and turn him from an innocent man into an imprisoned one.

Lust and law, Sarah thought to herself as her eyes darted back and forth between both men. *Those three words pretty much summarized this entire scandal and day.*

I couldn't describe this day any better than that, and as George declared minutes ago, the law won. The law squarely won, and I'm so glad it did.

THE END

Made in United States
Cleveland, OH
06 May 2025

16731129R00039